MOVE ON

MANJULA PAI

Contents

Contents

1

Is this a dream?

Dharini's eyes glanced at the words Sarson Ka Saag Makki Ki Roti. She kept the menu card aside and ordered her usual Paneer Parantha. She looked through her messages in her phone, there was nothing important or interesting.

Just then a man approached her and said 'Dharini ma'am'

Dharini was surprised, 'Aakash, is this a dream?'

'No, ma'am it's me, Aakash, the same Aakas who used to say Englis, now do you recognize me?'

'Yes.' Dharini thought how couldn't she. The most handsome man in the world according to her. Mascara eyes, a smile that could make her forget all her sorrows, the thick wavy black hair, the tanned and toned body, long legs and long hands, a sharp nose, juicy lips, hairy chest, the swag wala walk and the boyish voice. The man whom she had used as a muse for 5 of her novels and probably he was not even aware of it. She had never expected that they would meet each other again. But every time, she was writing a novel, she would think of him. Except for the dark circles under his eyes, a few strands of grey hair, a few wrinkles and a beard, he looked the same as his did years ago.

He saw Dharini and he too started thinking of the past. She looked the same except for a few wrinkles. Her short but curvaceous body, her thick jet-black hair, her big beautiful eyes and that smile that exposed her perfect teeth had made him fall for her a long time ago. His mentor, his motivator, his best friend -he asked himself. Was he still in love with her? Was it possible to be in love with someone for so long and realise it only when you meet that person again?

'Are you waiting for someone?'

'No, and you,'

'No, then may I join you'

'Sure'.

Aakash sat down.

'What are you doing in Mumbai?'

'Ma'am, I work as an information security director in an MNC, the one that is on this street. How about you?'

'I am working with a production company. They are producing a web series based on my novel. So, I have to be here for a few months.'

'How many kids do you have?'

'One son, he is 12. And you?'

'One daughter, 25, recently married.'

'How is your husband?'

'Must be fine' Aakash raised his eyebrows.

'The year after you moved to Mumbai, I got divorced, he left me for another woman.'

'My situation is the same, my wife left me for another man. I got divorced a few years ago.'

Dharini thought- 'What kind of a woman would leave someone like him?'

Their dishes arrived and they ate silently.

While leaving, Aakash asked, 'Do you come here often.?

'Yes, twice or thrice a week. I like it here- not too expensive, has a decent crowd and the food is so tasty.'

'Even I eat here once or twice a week, usually when I have to work beyond 6.'

'Ok, looking forward to meeting you again.'

'Same here.'

2
Twenty years ago

Aakash put on the TV and as usual watched wrestling. He liked the way people wrestled each other. Through them he too bashed some people whom he hated in his mind.

That night, he could not get his hate filled feelings. Instead, some positive feelings crept inside his mind.

He thought about his childhood. He belonged to a middle-class rural family. His parents had some acres of land where they farmed and through which they maintained the household. They were not rich but there was a lot of happiness. A father who would pat his back when he did something right. A mother who would hug him, kiss him and feed him on time. An elder brother who protected him from village bullies and a little sister who adored him. Apart from the family he had a lot of friends and a lot of pets-2 cows, 2 calves, a dog and a cat. There was no time to waste and no time to feel sad. He played and also studied well. He studied not for himself but to see the smile on his parents' face every time he did well in school. He was a class topper in 10th grade.

In 11th grade things changed because of a new girl in his class-Bela. Bela's house was on his street. His school was 4 kilometres away. Both of them cycled together. After a month Bela started acting weird. She asked him to take the short cut to school. It cut down the distance by half a kilometre but that stretch was lonely and also a mud road. She would sing Bollywood songs and often fall on him. And one fine day, she said 'I love you'. That day Aakash's boyhood said goodbye. It started with a kiss and within an year they were making love in the fields and in her room when no one else was there. Going to her room was an adventure. The terraces of their houses were well connected but he had to make sure that no one was watching while he went to her room. Her house was five houses away. Virginity of a woman was a big deal those days so they did only foreplay. He did not know how she felt but it was hell for him but at the same time he was addicted to love.

12th board exams arrived. This time, he just managed to pass. Studies, future and family-everything had taken a backseat because the only thing that mattered was Bela. With some jugaad, he had got a seat in a nearby degree college. He was going to do BSc computers. Bela had managed to get slightly better marks than him. He asked her to study in the same college. Unfortunately, she refused as she had other plans. Bela said and Aakash still remembered her words- 'I told my mother about us, she said we could not get married because in this village, there is a rule. Two people of the same village cannot get married. If we do, the villagers will kill us. 20 years ago, two lovers from this village, tried to elope. They were caught and buried alive under that big tree on the highway, near the bus stop. People say that their ghosts still haunt that tree. Please Aakash I love you but I don't want to die and I don't want to be a ghost. I am marrying a man whom my parents have chosen for me next month. I will be going to Rajasthan.

He works as a Panchayat secretary. I will always remember you. If you can, please forgive me.' For a whole month, he had cried himself to sleep.

Degree college life was good. Good marks, good friends and good fun.

After that, he did MCA. He got into one of the best colleges in Delhi. No jugaad was needed due to his good marks. Delhi life was good, first intro to city life and city girl. Pinky was as pink as her name. She was glamorous, sexy and bold. He never expected her to propose to him.

It was the same problem again-virginity clause. 'Let's save this for our wedding night' she said. After MCA, both Pinky and he got placed in a limited company as system admins. Within six months of his getting a job, Aakash's father passed away due to a massive heart attack. His brother through farming earned enough to run the household but did not have money to arrange for their sister's dowry. If their father was alive, somehow through his contacts, he would have arranged it. They could not let go of the alliance. The boy was a banker and a decent one. Aakash took the burden on himself by taking a loan to cover the dowry and marriage expenses. He decided to stay unmarried till he would repay the loan.

Two months after his sister's marriage Pinky broke up with him. Her parents had arranged her marriage with an NRI. This time too Aakash cried himself to sleep every day for a month.

Aakash laughed at himself. Due to these two girls, he was the one who was a virgin on his wedding night. He came to know only later that his wife was not one. He was not going to think of Soni that night. He was feeling good for once and he was not going to spoil it.

20 years ago, he had landed in Bangalore-city of dreams for every techie. But his experience of Bangalore was bad for the first year. Loneliness and cultural shock were what he had to face. Rice, Sambaar, Idli was something he found either too spicy or too sour for his taste. He would cook his meals to save money and time.

He enjoyed his work but he had no friends. Work, cook and eat-that's what his weekdays were. Sleep, wash clothes and buy groceries was what made up his weekends. Only source of entertainment he had was a portable TV.

One more thing that disappointed him were the girls. In North India, girls would just fall for his good looks. They rarely judged the way he dressed or the way he spoke English. Due to these two reasons, they avoided him so he could not date anyone.

The first day he met Dharini, he did not even bother to look at her properly. Sari clad, short women were not his type. But when she spoke those golden words, 'Aap kahan ke ho' he felt a rush of warmth and thus blossomed a great friendship. A month later he finally felt at home in Bangalore. He loved the city for three reasons-his job, the weather and Dharini. She had become his bestie.

When he was on the call floor or the training rooms, he would over hear people talking about Dharini.

'Ma'am is really cool. Can you ever imagine calling your English teacher by her first name.?'

'She even cracks some dirty jokes. Did you see how she says what the f and pauses?

'I expected a hot 'huduga' to be our English trainer but this lady is super.'

'Did you observe we have so much fun and at the same time we actually learn.?'

'Man, if she was 10 years younger, I would have proposed to her, what charm, what sense of humour.'

Whatever Akaash would overhear, he would tell Dharini. Her big, black eyes would become even bigger and she would laugh. A laughter that had no pretence, no control, just pure joy.

Suddenly, he realized that his key to happiness was just next to him and he was not using it to unlock his dreams. One afternoon when she was busy reading a novel, he asked- 'Ma'am, don't you have to prepare for your classes?'

'I am special, I just have to prepare for the first two classes for any new batch and after that even if you wake me up in the middle of the night, I can teach those topics.'

'What about paper corrections?

That's just once a week and those are objective questions so it only takes about two hours once a week to correct them.'

Ma'am can you teach me Englis for one hour every day.

I will ask boss's permission and we will start right away.

I hope its ok. I know you get 2 hours free time every day.

Why do you like your job Aakash?

I love to work with chords and the systems.

So that's your passion. Same here, teaching is my passion. It's also going to be a pleasure teaching you Mascara eyes.

Oh! That's what the ladies call you here. Do you know what is mascara?

Hanji, my Dilliwali girlfriend used to use it.

She asked the boss's permission and was back.

Okay, get ready for the 1st class with me Mascara eyes.

Since that day, for the next 3 months, Aakash was Dharini's student. Post lunch, they would spend one hour with each other. She would teach him grammar and polish his accent.

'It is not batter, it is better, batter is like dosa ka batter.'

'It is not Englis, it is English'

'Jaise shadi wala sh'

'Yes', Dharini blushed as she replied. That's when he realized how shy she was.

He was a diligent student and would seriously finish all the exercises and assignments. She too paid a lot of attention to his progress.

During these sessions, he used to observe little things about her-her perfect lips, her naughty eyes, her perfect teeth, her sweet smile and her big breasts.

He had started fantasizing about her and he felt that she too had a crush on him. The way she would avoid looking at his eyes. The slight pause in her speech when his hands would accidently touch hers.

He wanted to stop his feelings for her but he would just tell himself, 'As long as it was all within our hearts, it is Ok.' But as the days went by, his love for her increased.

One Sunday, after he had watched a Hindi movie in a theatre, he went inside a restaurant to have his lunch. As he waited for his food to arrive, he saw Dharini with her family. Thankfully she had not seen him. He saw her husband and he was jealous. The man looked as if he would probably wear formals even on weekend. He was sure that if he went close to him, he would smell a classic aftershave. He was clean shaved with hair neatly set.

Beside him, sat a cute five-year-old who looked like a smaller and a female version of her dad. Dharini was in a baby pink embroidered salwar suit. It was probably her husband's favourite because he had never seen her wear it to work. Aakash put on his sunglasses even though he was sitting indoors. He did not want Dharini to recognize him.

He saw Dharini looking at her husband once in a while but her husband was only talking to their child. For the first time he had seen Dharini in a different avatar-the avatar of a devoted mother. She looked so happy feeding her child. Her expressions were so natural and she seemed genuinely happy. He felt an even greater love and respect for her but at the same time he felt guilty. He was in love with a married woman and that too one who was a mother.

A week ago, his boss had told him that they were going to expand. They were going to start a 2000-seater call centre in Mumbai and his boss expected him to take care all the aspects relating to the computers and the phones, mainly take care of the networking. He decided he would take that offer because that would stop him from breaking Dharini's home.

As soon as he mentioned this to her, she was shocked. He remembered how her beautiful lips had parted. He wanted to kiss them badly but could not. After that, they purposely started avoiding each other. Two weeks later, the day arrived when he had to board his flight to Mumbai. The flight was in the evening and in the morning after completing some paperwork, he went straight to Dharini. He said, 'Ek hug to banta hai'

They hugged each other tightly. First time their bodies had touched. It tore his heart. Her breasts felt so soft and her hair smelt so good. He kissed her head and after that the embrace ended.

The sound of the wrestling match on TV brought him back to the present day. He decided it was time for him to share more hugs with Dharini.

3
Two decades ago

Once Dharini returned home, she started thinking of Aakash as he was 20 years ago.

It was her first day at Tring Tring, an international BPO. She was hired as a pre-process trainer. After finishing the joining formalities, she was asked to prepare for her upcoming training sessions which were scheduled the following week.

She was taken to the training department. A spacious place with spacious workstations. There were around 25 workstations and 2 cabins. She introduced herself to the other trainers who were there. Suddenly her eyes fell on the workstation next to hers. The table was empty but the floor was filled with chords. Out of curiosity, she asked the two young lady trainers who were present. 'Whom does the next pod belong to? Looks pretty empty for a trainer's table.'

'Oh! That one, it belongs to Mascara eyes.' Replied one of them.

'Oh, that is Dehati's 'said another and both started giggling. 'It belongs to a techie. Handsome hunk but can't speak English properly. Speaks only Hindi and that too it's so fast that we can't follow a single word that he speaks.'

After lunch, she was the only trainer in the department as others were busy with their classes.

An hour later, a man walked in and she stood up to greet him. He wore faded light blue jeans and an equally faded light blue denim shirt. He seemed to be in his own world. He dropped some chords on the floor and then as soon as he straightened himself, she said- 'Hi, I am Dharini, pre-process trainer and you?

'Aakas, system admin.'

She asked, 'Aap kahan ke ho?'

Suddenly his face brightened as he replied- 'Haryana'.

Dharini started speaking to him in Hindi. He started speaking really fast. As if, after he was silent for many days and since he had found someone to speak to, he was pouring his heart out. His Hindi was too fast but Dharini let him speak because she was dazed by his looks-wavy hair, fair skin which was slightly tanned, a sharp nose, dark pink lips and eyes as if mascara was applied to them. Eyes so beautiful and expressive, filled with secrets and pain that they glistened with dampness. 6 feet tall, a built so good that probably his shirt felt lucky touching him. Dharini felt some strange feeling starting at her mouth. It went down to her belly, she realized before it could go down any further, she had to stop it. So, instead of aaa aaa, she said- 'slow, slow'.

Aakash asked-Madam what?

'Please speak slowly. I didn't understand anything. Don't say madam instead say ma'am. Madam is Ok in British English but in American English, it is a bad word.'

'Ok Ma'am' and he smiled. What a beautiful smile he had, she thought. Dharini realized one thing, she found him so handsome that she could not look at him for more than a minute.

For the next one month whenever Aakash saw Dharini, he would talk to her. She felt as if she was not walking but hopping with joy like a school girl. He was so full of life. They would even have lunch together. One day, after a trip to his hometown, he had got her homemade besan laddoo. It was huge, well roasted, filled with desi ghee and was very tasty. But it was so heavy that after eating the laddoo, she could not eat her lunch.

One afternoon, as she sat reading a novel at her table, he approached her- 'Ma'am can you teach me Englis when you are free.'

Dharini took her boss's permission and the next day she started teaching Aakash. She taught him English for 1 hour every afternoon as she did not have classes during that time. She was amazed at his dedication and within months, he was as fluent in English as any other average Indian English speaker.

She loved his company but he made her want sex. She wanted her husband to fulfil that need but unfortunately, they had sex once a week, that too it was a quickie. She was also filled with guilt. She cursed herself for being unfaithful to her husband by fantasizing about another man. She and Aakash had never touched each other but she could feel that he was also developing feelings for her. He would look at her face and suddenly his gaze would travel to her neck and then to her breasts.

One incident still made her shiver. Some people constantly commented on his dressing sense.

'He repeats the same clothes'

'I think he has only 3 pairs.'

'Miser, can't spend on clothes.'

'Never seen him once in formals.'

'What a bore, spoils the ambience.'

'Spoke to him man to man also, he thinks only his good looks will work.'

Dharu was tired of hearing all these comments. Finally, she decided to speak to him.

'It's your birthday next week, right? Will I see you in formals?'

He looked at her and smiled, 'Yes, only for you I will be in formals.'

On his birthday, he was dressed in a black shirt and black pants. He looked really sexy. Instead of his usual deo, he had used an after shave that smelt really good. Dharini felt it again-the strange feeling go down her throat. She understood this time it was too much. She could not stop it. She excused herself and rushed to the washroom. She covered her mouth with one hand and held the towel stand with another. She climaxed and after that she felt relaxed. That night she held her Mangalasutra and cried. 'If only you had given me more time, this wouldn't have happened. I am sorry.' She said as if she was telling those words to her husband.

One day, Aakash said 'I am shifting to Mumbai. Dharini felt really upset but at the same time it was a good decision. Good for his growth and good for her guilt.

On the last day together, they spoke a lot and at last he said, 'EK hug to banta hai' and he gave her a tight hug.

There were a lot of people around them but bye-bye hugs were quite common. For the first time, their bodies had touched. He even kissed her head. After the hug, both of them felt like two teenage lovers who were separating from their first love.

Dharini sighed as she walked back to the present day from her memory lane.

Her faith in God had reduced considerably after her divorce. But that day, she thanked God wholeheartedly.

4

They meet again and again

2 days later, Aakash and Dharini met again at the little restaurant. They had dinner together.

Aakash asked- 'What are you doing this weekend?'

Dharini relied- 'Nothing much-sleeping, cleaning and writing.'

'Hey I know this place that sells awesome Golas.'

'Nahi, what if I fall sick'

'They use filtered water to make the Golas. If that makes you feel better.'

'That sounds good.'

'Saturday evening then.'

On Saturday evening, she wore a pair of jeans and a comfortable T-shirt and tied her hair in a high ponytail. She checked herself in the mirror. She was the kind who would not stand in front of a mirror for more than five minutes to look at herself. But that day she took five more minutes to look at herself.

They both had the red coloured Golas. Initially Dharini tried to take sips of the crushed ice ball but then she saw Aakash enjoying the Gola. His lips had turned red. They looked messy yet cute. She laughed and after that she too shamelessly ate the Gola like a school girl.

'There is a play called 'Tumhari Amrita' in one of the theatres. Do you want to see it?'

'My God! It's like a dream come true. I have been waiting to watch this play from such a long time.'

Dharini watched the play and Aakash watched Dharini. At the end of the play, Dharini's eyes were filled with tears.

After they came out of the theatre she said, 'I don't think this kind of love exists in this day and time'.

'Na mile, na dekha, na chua, phir bhi pyar kiya.'

'Maybe it does and only a handful of people had the luck to experience it

In the same week, on Friday evening Aakash called her. 'Hey, you know there is a karaoke bar where they play 90s ka songs. Let's check out that place tonight.'

They went to the bar. Dharini was happy to see that most people who were there were middle aged. Dharini managed to sing 4 songs in her not so melodious voice. Akaash too with great awkwardness managed to sing one song. He drank beer and she had a soft drink with a light dinner. They both had a long day at work but this experience made them feel really energetic. Dharini felt as if she was not walking but floating on air.

The next day, Aakash called her to have Golgappa

'I don't want Golgappa or Pani Puri. I want Puchka.

'Puchka?'

It is the same thing but the stuffing is different. You get it usually in Kolkatta. That's why I don't eat Golgappas here.'

'Ok I got it. There is a man who sells it near my place.'

Dharini ate 2 rounds of Puchkas. She forgot all her manners as she went on stuffing one Puchka after another in her mouth. Only taking a break to relish the masala filled water along with the potato and chana stuffing. It looked weird but Aakash enjoyed watching her eat. Her expressions were so different- as if she was going through foodgasm every time she ate her favourite dish.

Dharini do you like dancing?

I dance almost every day but only in my room.

'Let's go to a disco'

'Nahi, only youngsters will be there. I will feel uncomfortable.'

'Hey no, one of my building boys told me that there is an old disco where only oldies like us hang out.'

'Sounds good. Do you dance?'

'Not really. I only dance in Baraat.'

'I want to see your Baraatwala dance.'

'I know you dance well.'

'How?'

'Do you remember the party at Tring Tring?'

'Yes, the one that was held during our offsite.

'Ya, I remember how you let your hair down and danced as if no one was watching you. I want to see you like that again.'

'Maybe this time my moves won't be that quick.'

'Doesn't matter, you are a very graceful dancer and what matters is how we feel when we are dancing.'

Aakash was right. It felt great dancing with the disco lights and music.

Two weeks later both Dharini and Aakash were like besties. It was so good to have a friend of the opposite gender with whom you could have loads of fun.

Suddenly Dharini realized Aakash was doing all those things which she had mentioned in her poem. She knew if not already in love, Aakash was falling in love with her.'

5
Dharu gets drunk

On the following Saturday night, Aakash took Dharu to a beachside pub. They had a delicious dinner with whiskey. Dharini felt good after the first peg so she had another. But after the second peg, she started saying all those things which she usually told herself.

'Aakash let's walk on the beach.'

Aakash paid the bill and they started walking on the beach. Only a few people were on the beach and they were all far away from them. The pleasant beach air made her even more tipsy.

'Aakash don't wear black. I can't control myself when I see you in black. If you wear it again, I will fuck you.'

Aakash started laughing

'Hey why are you laughing. By the way, why did your wife leave you? Man leaves woman, everyone says 'ayyo papa'. But when woman leaves man, they laugh. Ok, don't start crying now.'

Aakash was silent. Dharu touched his forehead. 'No problem with this-smart techie.'

Then she kept her hand on his chest and said, 'This is also good. What a heart.'

After that, she slid her hand down and pulled his belt. 'So, the problem is below this. I want to find out one day.'

She took his hand and kissed it. 'You know what someone wrote about me-Love less writer writes love stories. Yes, I have no lover in my life but that does not mean that I don't want to be loved. I always want the man to make the first move. Maybe that's why my husband left me because I am not good at expressing my feelings. Just look at this situation, what a beautiful place and what a handsome man. I don't even have the guts to kiss those juicy lips.'

Aakash held her arm tightly this time as she was losing her balance. 'I don't know why my husband left me. I have heard it from that stick but never directly from him. I have never asked him as I am scared that I will hear what I don't want to. I don't love him anymore but I feel that he left me because I was ugly. I can see the proof now. I am walking with you alone on this beautiful night and you don't even desire me.'

Aakash could not control himself anymore. He hugged her tightly and kissed her cheek. 'No, that's not true Dharu, I am madly in love with you.'

Suddenly, she pushed him and said, 'Take me to my place right now and don't touch me.'

He was shocked but decided before she shouts again and attracts other people's attention, it would be better that he dropped her home.

He drove as fast as he could and reached her apartment. He somehow managed to get the keys out of her bag, made her remove her shoes and made her sleep on the bed. Then he asked her to go to sleep.

'I will not give my body for free. It has been untouched for years. There is a price for this.'

Aakash was stunned when he heard her talking like a slut. But he smiled when he heard her next line and left.

'The price of this body-love, lots of love.'

He was confused and stressed. He decided never to tell her about this incident as he knew dignified Dharu would be ashamed of herself. He was also happy at the same time as he understood that she too loved him.

6

Confessions

It was 7 in the evening and Wednesday, Dharini had removed her make up, showered and was in her favourite T shirt and leggings. She put on her playlist on TV, when the doorbell rang. She wondered who it could be because she hardly knew anyone in the city other than her colleagues, few friends and relatives. If they dropped in, they would usually call before they dropped in.

She opened the door and found Akaash standing at the door in black formal shirt and striped trousers. 'Oh, not black again' she thought. He looked so handsome in black. Wish she could wear her sunglasses in the house too. That way she could stare at him guilt free.

'Hi Aakash, come in'

'Is it Ok, it is raining and Mumbai rains, you know it may not stop for an hour or so. I thought I will drop in for some gup shup. Are you busy?'

'No, not at all. I just came in an hour ago. Was planning to make some pakoras and chai.'

'Wow rains and pakoras. It's been so long since I had some home-made pakoras.

Make yourself comfortable. It's my playlist. All sad love songs. You can stop it and watch something else on the TV.

Its Ok

You may get bored

I like sad songs nowadays.

Ok I am hungry. I will quickly make the pakoras.

Do you want me to help you?

No, I don't like men in the kitchen.

Why?

They make tasty stuff but they mess up the kitchen.

He laughed a little and his eyes twinkled.

After fifteen minutes, Dharini brought a plateful of pakoras and placed it on the little table in front of Aakash.

'Here are your hot pakoras, I will go get the chai.'

She looked at Aakash as there was no reply. On TV the song 'Koi ye kaise bataye ki woh tanha kyun hai' was playing. Tears were streaming down Aakash's handsome face and falling on his trousers. His big beautiful eyes had turned red and she realised he had been like this for at least 5 minutes. She stood next to him and put her hand on his shoulder, he was shaking and she could hear his sobs. Suddenly he hugged her and kept his head on her breasts and cried uncontrollably. She too hugged him and caressed his thick, soft strands of hair. After five minutes, his crying stopped and so did the hugging.

'I am sorry, I usually cry alone but today I could not control it'

'It's OK. Wash your face, eat the pakoras. They will soon become cold.'

Dharu looked at him as he got up. Her breath became heavy as she clenched her fist. His tearful face made him look strangely attractive. After some time, he came and sat on the sofa and took a pakora. 'Tastes so good. Feel like kissing the hand that made them.' He said that and gave her a naughty smile.

'So, now Mr Akaash is on flirt mode, I suppose. Alright, I will cancel chai and get some whiskey instead. We will order some dinner later. Till then we shall only drink and speak. Ok?'

'Thanks Dharini.'

Over pakora and whiskey, he poured his heart out. His eyes were filled with tears again- 'I don't know how she could leave me. I loved her so much. I miss my son. She is not letting me have his custody. I miss my little boy.'

'I think you should move on. Find someone, get married and start another family.'

'I can't. I have failed.'

That does not mean you will fail again.

'I don't want any more kids.'

'You should have a woman in your life at least.'

'I have tried Dharu, may I call you Dharu.'

'Yes, you may.'

I have dated two women. One, a model, half my age and another, a serial actress, few years younger than me. Both these relationships did not work because they felt I was emotionally unavailable and a workaholic.'

'Dharu, I need a mature woman in my life- a soul mate. I need someone with a beautiful mind. I have had enough of beautiful bodies with empty souls.'

'I am tired of being a giver-give money, give advice, give satisfaction in bed, just give, give and give till I lose everything. I want to take now. I can provide financially and sexually but emotionally; I have lost everything.' Again, he started crying. This time, he put his head on her lap and cried. Without thinking much, she kissed his head. He took her fingers and kissed them between his sobs.

He got up, wiped his tears, took a few sips of whiskey and again started speaking.

'I love you, Dharu. I need you in my life.'

When he said this, she just froze.

'I know you feel the same about me. I knew it 20 years ago. I felt the same way. I know that the character, Gagan is me. You gave Gagan a nick name, 'Mascara eyes', that's what you called me back in those days.

She turned towards him to say something but she remained silent. She, a woman who could play with words as if they were toys in her novels, her poems and speeches, was at a loss of words. She quickly took two sips of her drink.

You just changed the relationship in the novel- Gagan was your student whereas I was your colleague. You have never looked at my eyes and so hasn't Gagan's teacher Disha.

You didn't look at me directly years ago and even now you don't. You look at me only when you think I am not looking at you. I sensed it the other day when we went out and you hardly removed your sunglasses. It is because you find me attractive.'

Her head reeled due to the fact that he had confessed about his feelings for her and also because he knew that she too loved him.

'I have read that novel of yours 10 times-twice after we met in Mumbai. I too loved you Dharu when you were in Tring Tring but I had to control my feelings because I didn't want to break your home.'

'Look at my face Dharu, please.'

She turned towards him and for the first they looked into each other's eyes and within no time, their lips were locked in a long kiss. The kiss was so good that Dharu felt she would end up making love to him. She quickly pulled herself away.

'Do you love me, Dharu?'

'Yes, I love you, Aakash.

They hugged and her head was on his chest and she could hear his heart beat and nothing else.

After that she returned to her senses. 'I think both of us are drunk today.'

'Dharu I am a middle-aged man not a school boy who gets drunk after having a peg.'

'Maybe, I am drunk. I will just order food.'

Aaskash was shocked at her detached behaviour.

'What do you want?'

'I need something heavy, pizza and another glass of whisky.'

She ordered the pizza and till it arrived, she dimmed the lights, the song, 'Ajeeb dastan hai yeh' was playing on TV. He held out his hand, she put her head on his broad shoulders.

'I know it happened so fast. Chal koi na, take your time and then let me know if you want this relationship. We can start by becoming friends with benefits.'

'I want this relationship Aakash but I want you to think about us seriously. I have finished most of my responsibilities. But think practically, I am a middle-aged woman, 5 years older than you. Soon I will have lots of wrinkles and my body will sag. You are much better looking than me. And if we continue this after I leave Mumbai, it would be a long-distance relationship. Will you be able to manage this?If your answer is a yes, then come tomorrow for dinner.' They silently watched some more songs and then had their dinner.

While leaving, Aakash kissed her hand and said, 'Tomorrow, order Rajma chawal and Rabdi. I will be here.'

'Let's see, Mr Handsome.'

'You will, Miss Beautiful Heart.'

'Please, this lioness hasn't had sex for 2 decades. If you stay a little more, I will go wild with lust and you won't be able to control me.'

'That sounds dangerous, bye lioness.'

7

It's a yes

Dharini woke up next morning. She felt she should stay at home that day but decided against it. Firstly, that day they were shooting an important scene and secondly if she stayed at home, the previous evening's scene would replay in her mind again and again. Even the thought about his answer would make her even more restless.

As soon as she returned home that evening, she ordered their dinner so that when they were together there would be no disturbance. She then showered, wore a light green dress as green clothes brightened her face and she considered it lucky. She applied a little more make up than usual. She was usually very hungry every evening but somehow the anxiety had killed her hunger. She put on a channel that showed documentaries as that would distant her mind from reality. She decided to wait for him till 8 and then change her clothes and wear her dull but comfortable night wear. Half an hour passed, there was no sign of him.

Exactly at 7.30, the bell rang and her heart beat increased. She ran to open the door but paused. She should not behave like a teenager in love. She took a deep breath before she opened the door. He was there-with a box of chocolates in one hand and a bouquet of red roses in another.

She softly said 'come in.' and quickly closed the door. He gave her the roses and the chocolates. Both of them just looked into each other's eyes for a minute. She kept the gifts on the table. He took her hand in his and said, 'It's a yes from me'.

He slowly took her to the sofa and they kissed. She kissed his eyes, his nose, his cheeks and he received all these kisses with closed eyes. He kissed her neck and bent her slightly and started to kiss more while trying to make her lie down on the sofa. Suddenly, she stopped him.

'Please stop, I want this to be special. I haven't slept with anyone for almost 20 years.'

'I am sorry, you must be thinking that I am cheap and fast.'

'No, the other reason is that I haven't waxed my legs and I look like a bear.'

'I don't care. I love your soul so I can love you with your hairy legs.'

'Aakash let's not make love in my place. I will feel really sad when you go away. Saturday night at your place.'

'Ok as you wish but can I at least kiss a few more times before I go my girlfriend.'

'Yes, you can my boyfriend.'

8
They visit a temple

The next afternoon, Dharu called Aakash – 'Can you come home this evening?'

'Can't wait till tomorrow, can you?'

'Cheee, no I want to visit a temple.'

'What? Ok, shall we go to the Durga temple near your house?

'No, take me to a Krishna temple. Only Kanha ji will understand me.'

'Sure Dharu, as you wish.'

Dharini draped a Bandhini saree-a red coloured one that evening.

Aakash arrived and he said, 'Wow! Dressed like a bride in red. We are visiting a temple anyway, shall we get married.'

'Oh! Please stop joking.'

'Can I kiss you?'

'No, please let's go. I hope Krishna forgives me.'

Suddenly the smile vanished from Aakash's face. 'Forgive me? What are you guilty of Dharu? For god sake move on. We are not having an extra marital affair. We are both divorced. Relax and enjoy this. This is not adultery. What our spouses did was adultery. If you want to pray, let's ask Krishna to bless our union. Ask him for happiness. Pray that we are together now and forever. That is what I am going to ask him.

Silently, they travelled to the temple. In front of the idol, both prayed wholeheartedly for their new found togetherness.

After that, they went to the little Indian restaurant, the place they had first met each other in Mumbai. Aakash ordered 'Mooli Ke Paranthe'. The waiter looked at her and said, 'Didi, Paneer Parantha.' She smiled and said, 'Bhayya Nahi, Sarson Ka Saag, Makki Ki Roti.'

Aakash dropped her home but she asked him not to come to the door.

'Khud ko rok nahi payenge.'

'I won't be able to stop myself. Just wait for one more night. Let this be special.'

9
Treasure of pleasure

It was their first night together. Initially it was awkward for both of them as Dharu was shy and scared. It was so long since she had slept with a man that she felt like a virgin again. Aakash was very patient and gentle. After the love making session, they quietly lay down beside each other. Aakash put on the TV in his bedroom and they watched some Bollywood love songs.

After an hour, Dharu felt a wave of strength in her. She turned to Aakash and said- 'In round one, you were active and I was passive. In round two we will reverse the roles'

Aakash said- 'Dharu no grammar exercises in bed ok.'

Dharu replied- 'It's sexercise my toy boy. Just relax and trust me.'

Aakash did exactly that and Dharu was the one who satisfied him. After it ended Aakash genuinely said- 'Wow that was great. I have never felt this way before'

'You know Aakash one of the things that kept me going during these sexless years- fantasies. I don't know how long our affair is going to last so every time we have sex, I am going to try something new. It is not only going to bring me happiness but you will feel as if you are sleeping with a different woman each time. I will try and make it that good for you. Are you ready for this adventure?

Of course, Dharu I am.

Aakash felt a new sense of pride that night. The whole world knew Dharu as a dutiful, nurturing and ethical woman. He was the only one who knew that behind closed doors she was a treasure of pleasure.

10
Her daughter knows

Dharini reached Bangalore on Friday morning and by 11, she was at Tanya's place for her first Tulsi pooja. She saw her daughter in a beautiful magenta silk saree, looking prettier than before. Her flawless skin was glowing and so was the face of her son-in-law. She helped her daughter bind small bundles of grass and flowers in a certain way and also arranged all the other items required for the pooja and then stepped away from the Tulsi plant. It had been so many years since she had last performed this pooja meant exclusively for married women. Tanya's mother-in-law asked her to join the ceremony but she refused politely saying that she had forgotten most of the rituals. Tanya and the rest of the married women present performed the ritual. There were around 25 guests, mostly women. Even her sister was there. She chatted with everyone, had lunch and was the first one to leave the place as she was really tired and also because she was afraid if the news of her Mumbai affair had reached Bangalore.

The next morning, her daughter arrived. Everything was going on well till evening. After tea her daughter said, 'I want to show you some pics'.

There were two-first one Aakash and her laughing. The next one shocked Dharu-it was raining and both their heads were hidden in Aakash's jacket. It was the famous pose from one of the 90s movies. She remembered; it hadn't been intentional. Both he and Aakash had forgotten to carry umbrellas. It had started raining heavily so Aakash had taken his jacket to cover both their heads. They had kissed under it as the rain and their wet bodies had made them forget that they were in public.

'What is this Ma? Lucky's cousin who lives in Mumbai sent this to him. Thank God he had the good sense not to send it to anyone else in the family. What's wrong with you? Why can't you be like other moms? Sharu aunty was asking if you will accompany her as she is going to travel to several holy places after two months. If you are lonely find something meaningful to do. Lucky feels you are going through mid-life crisis. The guy is too handsome. He may be a flirt. Found you lonely and available so he is just hooking up with you. He will leave you in no time. He must be a fuck boy for all you know.

Tanya continued- 'I have seen you hit rock bottom after your divorce. I don't want to see you like that again.'

Dharu said- 'I won't lie to you. I was lonely after your marriage. He too is a divorcee like me.'

'Is he younger than you?'

'Yes, five years younger.'

'See, don't get me wrong Ma. I am not saying that I expect you to be single for the rest of your life. After your divorce, you made me your purpose of life. I want you to live for yourself now. Ma, I feel that he is too good for you that's why he will ditch you. Please think about it.'

'I will'.

11

She meets his colleagues

Dharini finished her work early so she decided to meet Aakash. He invited her to his workplace.

'Why don't you come here? I am sure some of your fans will be thrilled to take selfies with their favourite writer.'

'Come on, techies and books'

'Dharu, you don't know how many techies read novels during their free time.'

'I will be there not only to take selfies with my fans but also to see my hottie being a bad ass boss.'

'You are most welcome my dear'

Once she reached the place, Aakash came near the entrance to receive her. The place looked like a typical MNC-false ceilings, glass doors, wall to wall carpet, AC, neat and tidy.

He took her to the cafeteria. Only few people were there. It was around 5.30 in the evening. The shift would end at 6 so the place was empty.

'I will just grab some coffee for you.' He got a cup of coffee from a machine. Then said- 'I just have to send a couple of emails, conduct a short debriefing session and then I will be back'

'It's OK, take your time. It is usually you who waits for me. Let me wait for you once in a while.'

Their eyes met. They both smiled-a special smile which flashed on both their faces, only when they were with each other. A smile that signalled love.

After he left, three girls walked in and started talking.

'Hey I heard Khadoos has got his girlfriend to office today.'

'Khadoos has a girlfriend. Poor you, heart-broken, that's why I tell you don't fall for these uncles when there are so many boys to choose from.'

'Khadoos is so mature, responsible and a workaholic'

'That's why probably his wife left him.'

'No, Khadoos can never be faulty. His wife was a cheater.'

'At least now stop hitting on him.'

'Ok now I will hit on Tabbu from Accounts department.

'Again, a man over 40. What's your problem? Do you have daddy complex?'

'Hmmm, at least Tabbu is single not divorced with a kid.'

'Babes, I am really curious to know who his current girlfriend is.'

'Must be some emotionally unavailable, sexy person like him.'

'I heard she is a writer. Writers are full of emotions right.'

'You can never say. Maybe she reserves all her emotions for her books. I am sure she will be short haired, khadi salwar kameez with chunky terracotta jewellery types.'

Dharini had no choice but to listen to them while sipping her coffee, as they were sitting at the next table and were speaking loudly. She understood that they were talking about Aakash and her.

'Who is that lady?' asked one of the girls looking at Dharu.

'That aunty must be some project manager or director's wife. The kurti she is wearing looks elegant and expensive. Hubby earning well, wifey spending well.'

Dharu wondered how quickly people could judge others.

It was 6 PM. Dozens of people walked into the cafeteria. Suddenly 4 people approached Dharu.

One of them said 'Ma'am selfie please. You are so simple and you seem to be a sorted person. Can't imagine you are the one who writes about guns and gangsters.'

Dharu said- 'It's all in my imagination dear. You don't need to commit a murder to write about murders.'

Another one added- 'I have read all your books and watched all the web series based on them'

Thank you, it is because of fans like you that make writers like me write more.

A guy joined them and said- 'Aakash is my boss. You have changed him Ma'am. He is less strict with us nowadays.' After that the group took a selfie with her.

Some more people started taking selfies with her.

Suddenly Aakash came and grabbed her hand and turned to the group.

'Sorry guys she will be back in two minutes'

'Meet my boss Dharu'

'Hello'

'Now I know the reason why this eternally sad looking chap seems happy now. Please continue to do this magic on him.

'Thank you but the truth is he too has changed me'

'Wow, rare to find this kind of love nowadays. '

After some small talk, some more people took selfies with Dharu. Then the three girls who were previously gossiping about her, appeared.

'Ma'am we are sorry if what you overheard has hurt you.'

'It's Ok. I know so many things about Aakash now.'

'And Ma'am it was just a crush.'

'It's Ok dear, the heart does not ask your permission before it starts crushing on someone.'

'Ma'am, you are the writer of my favourite web series and I failed to recognize you.'

'It alright dear. So many of us who work behind the scenes are never known so it's nothing new.'

'But how is it that we can connect with your stories.'

'I have a daughter who is around your age.'

'So ----Aakash is younger than you.

'Yes'

'You are a trendsetter then'

'Thanks for calling me that. Why should only men date younger women? Women should also date younger men if they want to. '

'One selfie Ma'am'

They took a selfie with her and left. After a little small talk with some more colleagues of Aakash, both of them went to the basement. Just when Dharu was going to get into the car, a young man in his twenties requested her for a selfie.

'Ma'am a selfie please. My aunt will really like it. After my dad's death, she looked after our family. So, she remained single. Recently, she read your novel, got motivated by it and has started dating this really nice man.

After taking a selfie with him, Dharu sat inside the car. Aakash smiled at her and said- 'You are a celebrity my dear.'

'Just a small one'

'But more than that I like the fact that so many women are getting inspired to move on after reading your book'

'Thank you, Khadoos'.

'That stupid girl must have told you about the nickname that I have in the office'

'Which one? The one that has a crush on you. Why did you reject her?'

'Please, such an immature girl. I need a woman who can take care of my son and me. If I marry someone like her, I will end up babysitting two kids.'

So Khadoosji please smile

'Hanji my dear writer ma'am.'

12

The muse

───────•♡•───────

Dharini, do you have a muse? The same looks, the same description. Your readers and our viewers are going to get bored of this. Looks like you are stuck in the 90s. People want variety these days. Why can't the hero be someone who looks like those guys from the world-famous boy band. Or someone who looks like dark chocolate or at least make the character have a nice trimmed beard like the style that is trending nowadays. At this rate we will only be popular with the TV audience.' Shouted Ali, the director of the web series.

'Please try to understand, apart from a writer you are also a business woman. The youth is your biggest audience so try to write something that attracts them and something that can attract the OTT audience worldwide. And who falls in love without touching each other. Sounds so old fashioned. I have fallen in love a few times but not unless I have banged the woman a few times. Don't get me wrong, your content is Ok but people need to connect with it. So, is your next novel also an uncle aunty love story?'

'No, it's an aunty youngster love story.' Tears had filled Dharu's eyes.

'Alright, looks like you got the message.' Said Ali calming down.

'Don't worry, one of us will help you with the hero's description, you focus on the story. Take the afternoon off, you can join us in the evening.' Said the producer.

'Thank you'

Dharu went to the washroom and cried.

After that, she sat in an empty room and messaged Aakash.

Hi are you busy

No, why?

Nothing

Dharu, please tell me what is troubling you. You rarely text me when I am at work.'

I am sorry. I didn't mean to disturb you.

I will take a day off.

Please don't, its nothing important.

You are important to me. Where are you?

At the studio.

Dharini cried some more, then washed her face and applied her make up.

Aakash was at the studio exactly half an hour later. He got out of his car and without even bothering who was looking at them, gave Dharu a tight hug and kissed her head.

Half the film crew saw this. Dharu waved her hand at them and left. Aakash drove to her place.

Once they reached her place, she narrated the incident to him- 'Aakash, am I abnormal? I don't seem to find any other man attractive other than you.'

'Same here, I don't find any other woman attractive other than you. That's because what's between us is not attraction but love.'

'See, Dharu neither Ali is wrong nor you. It's just that you both were born at different times. In our days, I did not even speak to any girl in my class and nowadays people are chatting away with strangers who are from different countries.'

'Your last novel 'Guns, girls and gangsters' was different. So, it does not mean that you can't think differently. It's just that you need to understand the tastes of viewers. Watch the shows that are popular, read the bestsellers, talk to your daughter, hang out with youngsters. I will also get you connected with my younger colleagues. They will be more than happy to help you with their opinions. I am sure you will be able to write more youthful stories.'

'Thank you Aakash.'

'Yaar, phir se thank you. The next time you think of saying sorry or thank you, kiss me when we are in private and flash that beautiful smile of yours when we are in public. Feeling better or shall we do something else.'

'I won't let your day off go wasted. Aakash make love to me so passionately that I forget everything that happened this morning.'

He did so and after that both of them fell asleep. When they woke up from their post sex nap both of them felt really hungry.

'Dharu let us have lunch at that restaurant where they treat us like a king and a queen. Then you can have chocolate sundae and I will eat Gud Bud ice cream.

Post lunch and ice cream, Aakash said- 'Nothing is better than food and sex.'

'You are right, hottie.'

They walked and talked in a park. Around five in the evening, Dharu went home and got ready for work. She wore the pink, sleeveless kurti that he had gifted her along with a dark blue pair of leggings. He couldn't take his eyes away from her short yet shapely legs. He was crazy about her curves.

He dropped her off at the studio. The story discussion began that evening and suddenly Trishna said- 'Hick, hick, hickey.' Looking naughtily at Dharu. Dharu blushed and looked down at her feet.

Ali too smiled at her- 'Is that your boyfriend?

'No, just friend.'

'Friends with benefits?'

Dharu blushed again and looked away.

Ali continued- 'The muse'

'Yes, the muse'

13
Friends with benefits

Aakash and Dharini came out of a literary event. Dharini was very happy as she had won the year's – 'Best story writer award.' Aakash too was happy for her achievement.

Just when they were about to get into his car, parked in the basement, two men came towards them. One a handsome young man and another a handsome middle-aged man. The young man started to speak to Dharini- 'He is the one you chose, why not me? Such a big event and you chose him over me.' Dharu held the young man's elbow as if to calm him down while the other man added, 'You didn't even bother to tell me.'

'Guys, I didn't tell Aakash either. He managed to get a pass for the event from one of the organizers to surprize me.'

'You love surprizes, don't you slut.'

Immediately Aakash held the young man's collar and the other man slapped him.

'Please stop it Rahil.'

Rahil ran his fingers through her hair and said, 'I am sorry, this was the first time I saw you with another man and I couldn't control myself.'

'Ok guys, let's not create a scene here and spoil my big day. Aakash please take us to our favourite restaurant.' It was a restaurant with retro décor and music. The tables were in cabins so it gave a lot of privacy to the customers especially lovers. They all sat inside one of the cabins.

'I know let's have something to eat.' After they had ordered, Rahil started talking 'Dharu tell us today, whom do you like the most?

'Guys, I have told you before, I don't have favourites. I like you all. You guys are special in your own ways.

Rahil, you with your virgin like innocence makes me feel youthful again.

Aakash-you are my muse. Alpha male in whose arms I feel so safe.

Sagar-you are my go-to person with whom I can speak about anything ranging from politics to porn. My soulmate, my therapist.

Rahil, I think you need to hang out with girls your age.'

'So that, they can cheat on me just like my ex did,' said Rahil

'Not all women are cheaters, Rahil.' Said Dharu.

'Dharu I need you. Why didn't you wear my mom's necklace?'

'They had a dress code at the event'

Rahil kissed her on the cheek, Aakash banged the table and Sagar looked away.

'These men will die before you. I will take care of you just the way you took care of me when I was a child.'

Hearing this, both Aakash and Sagar looked at each other.

'Please marry me Dharu'

'Rahil you are exactly half my age. You are 25 and I am 50.'

'I don't care. I love you and that's the only thing that matters to me'

By then, the food was served.

'Ok, we will talk about that later. First be a good boy and finish your food.'

All of them ate silently. Once in a while, Rahil would take spoons of food and feed Dharu. When he did this, he would say- 'Eat na, babushona'

Aakash and Sagar with great difficulty managed to suppress their laughter whenever he did this.

After they had finished eating, Sagar paid the bills.

'Ok let's go.' Said Dharu

Where are you going? asked Rahil.

To my house

With which one of us?

Rahil, I am too tired so I want to be alone.

Tomorrow is Sunday and you are going to spend the whole day with me.

Fine.

They dropped Rahil first and after that they decided to go to a bar and drink to calm their nerves.

As soon as they reached the bar, Dharu made a call- 'Just make sure that he takes one of those green pill Kano. Don't leave him alone and I will be there by 10 tomorrow.'

Aakash shouted, 'Psycho'

'Please, don't be so rude. He has PTSD. He has seen his mother hanging and seen his ex with his friend making out in his own room. His dad only sends him money and rarely visits him. Thankfully, his best friend lives with him. His therapist says in another two months, he should be fine. Guys, I am tired of playing double roles-mother and lover. But I have to save that child. Ok let's talk about you guys now.'

Dharu continued- 'Ok, he is a kid but you both acted as if you were about to beat each other up. I told you that this is a casual relationship. Your egos got hurt when you saw me with another man. I have clearly told you that I date a guy only for 6 months and break up but I don't know why you guys want to still be with me even after 6 months. I am a healer. I heal with my love and then move on.

'I don't want to be healed' Said Aakash

'Same here' added Sagar.

'But just stay away from Rahil. He is dangerous. You may get killed Dharu.'

'Just give me two months guys'

Aakash looked at Sagar and said- 'Sir, I hate you.'

'So do I'

'I am going to Mumbai; I hate to say this to you but please take care of her.'

'I will Mr.Aakash.'

Aakash started crying and saying- 'Dharu don't do this, please, I love you.'

'Aakash what happened? I am right here. Utho Aakash , ankhen kholo.'

Aakash opened his eyes and he realised; it was a dream. He hugged her and then asked her 'Dharu, when you mentioned friends with benefits in your poem, did you mean you want more friends like me'

'Are you crazy? You are the only lover I have had in all these years. How can you even talk like this? Friends means friend plus friend =me + you. You are the only one I have and even if we break up, I will live with your memories for the rest of my life.'

'You are also my one and only, Dharu-now and forever.'

She looked at the little alarm clock on the bed side table and said- 'Its 2. Please let's go back to sleep. Both of us have a long day tomorrow. But I think I am going to need my sleeping pill'

'I will give it to you'. After that they made love even more passionately than before as if to prove that the love, they had for each other was eternal.

14

I don't want this world

Dharu's dating life was going on smoothly until one weekend. A whole weekend had passed with no messages, no phone calls. Dharu felt hurt that Aakash had chosen to break up with her by ghosting her. She tried to calm herself by thinking that the reason could be some major issue at work or his village had occured, that is why he was not contacting her.

On Monday, as usual she went to work. She thought he just needed a small break. That evening, she was really worried so she called his friend Raghu.

'Raghu, is there too much work in the office? Aakash hasn't contacted me from past two days.'

'Actually, he left office on Friday afternoon. He got a call from his mother. His wife delivered a baby boy that morning. He just asked me to take care of things here and rushed out. His eyes were filled with tears. I tried calling him too but he hasn't picked my calls since then.'

After this, Dharu messaged Aakash.

If you don't call me now, I am coming to your place.

After five minutes, she received his call and he said-'Please leave me alone. I don't want to talk to anyone. I don't want this world.' Then he cut the call.

His tone suggested that he had been crying and drinking. But what scared Dharu the most were his words-I don't want this world.

She called Raghu and narrated the incident. She added-'I am going to his place now. Please come there as soon as you can because if he tries to harm himself, I alone won't be able to stop him.'

When she reached his place, she rang the bell, after what seemed a long time, he opened the door. He looked sick-he had not shaved or bathed for 2 to 3 days. His beautiful eyes looked tired and red. They had lost their spark. This was the first time she had seen him so negligent.

Once inside the house, she hugged him but he pushed her away. She held his hand and made him sit on the bed next to her. Suddenly, he put his head on her lap and cried like a baby. 'My little Ved is going to be neglected even more. That bitch has 3 sons now and I want only one-my Ved. I want my baby. I miss him.' He spoke some other things in his native language. As the language was similar to Hindi, Dharu could understand most of the things that he said.

Once he sat, Dharu said- 'We will get him back. Meet her and talk to her about this. Let us think logically. She has just delivered a baby. After 3 to 4 months, go meet her and ask her for your child.'

By then, Raghu had arrived. He gave him a hug and said-'Bro, C'mon man up'

'What had happened?' Dharu asked this as she felt that if he spoke, the hidden emotions could be released and he would feel better.

'For the first four years of our arranged marriage, everything seemed fine. I got an onsite opportunity so I had to go abroad for an year. I left her and my son in her parent's place. Saajan was her neighbour's cousin and he was staying in her village to sort out some property matters. My son's play school was about 4 kilometres away so he started dropping her and my son to school. Soon they fell in love and had an affair. The day I reached India after my project, she ran away with him and also took my son with her. I wanted to beat him up but her brother stopped me. I still remember his words- 'Jiju, I got the news that Saajan has purchased a local gun. So, I request you to leave my sister alone as three lives in danger-hers, Ved's and the baby in her tummy. She is two months pregnant.'

Aakash continued- 'My whole world crashed in front of me. Not only had my wife had an affair but also, she was pregnant with that man's child. Saajan is actually a handsome and rich gangster. It was mainly his money that attracted my wife. She always wanted a luxurious life and I failed to give her that. Saajan used some jugaad and we got divorced the next day.

I meet Ved whenever I can. He is provided all the basic necessities and also with all those toys and gadgets a boy of his age wishes for. He also has a man servant to take care of him. The only thing he lacks is love. Though his mother is too busy with her lavish life, second husband and second son, she does not want to give me his custody. She thinks society will judge her even more for being a bad mother. This the biggest tragedy of my life.'

'Don't worry Aakash, we will try every possible trick under the sun to unite you and your son.'

Raghu said- 'I am sure she will help you Aakash, just get your confidence back.'

'Yes, I will. Thanks both of you for saving my life.'

'I won't let you die ahead of me, hottie.' Dharu said.

Both the men smiled at this dialogue.

15

Aakash wants to marry her

For the next two weeks, except for the time they were at work, Dharu took care of Aakash in every possible way. Most of the days either she stayed at his place or he was at hers. She made sure that he would be happy. She spoke to him most of the time, used her sense of humour to make him laugh, cooked his favourite dishes and made him super happy in bed. The result was amazing, he was not sad anymore. Aakash understood that he needed her in his life so one night when they were together, he told her, 'Let us get married, Dharu.'

Dharu was shocked.

Dharu was really happy but she thought practically, 'I need some more time Aakash. If we get married, for me it will be the best thing. You have all the things that I desire in a man-handsome, awesome in bed, responsible, caring, kind, mature. You are 5 years younger than me that's why I can see that you naturally tend to respect me. A woman wants not only love but also respect at my age. You are good in money matters. You are an ideal family man. Both of us are madly in love with each other but Aakash it should be a win-win situation. In a moment of desperation, you get married to me and then after 5 years, you should not regret it. In case you leave me for a younger woman I don't know what will happen to me. My divorce has broken me, one more divorce and I will get shattered completely. So please let us not rush into things.'

'I want you not only as my wife but also as Ved's mother. I need your help in bringing him up. You have been a single parent and you have done such a good job with Tanya; I am sure you will be an equally good parent to Ved.'

'Aakash, Ved is a boy. I haven't brought up boys. My sister has two sons and they are like chalk and cheese- so different. One does not want to stay at home and the other does not want to leave his room. I also need a little more time so that I can prepare myself for raising your son. I know I can be quite good at it because I was a step child myself so I know what are the things a child expects in a stepmom. But please thodi time aur do.'

'Aakash one more thing-I can't give up writing romances.'

'Who asked you to? I may be from a rural background but that does not make me conservative. Sometimes, I feel city people are more conservative than us. For example, in my village, there are at least ten women who are older than their husbands and they are happier than most other couples.'

'Will you accept a 25 years old woman as your daughter?'

'In my village, there are a lot of men who were victims of child marriage, they have grand children now. Just the other day, one of my friends grand-son called me 'Dadaji'. Yes, I can accept your daughter as my daughter.'

'I am actually not a perfect homemaker. You may have seen that. I still can't make gol gol rotis. I can't drape a saree properly. After one hour, I am usually stamping on the pleats or the saree is so high that my feet are visible. So many things like this, I am more of a tomboy.'

Aakash laughed- 'It's Ok Dharu, no one is perfect. I will buy you a roti maker and you don't have to wear sarees in public anymore. I will buy you lehengas. But put on a saree once in a while even if it is not so well draped. Sarees look so good on you, Uff your curves Dharu, stand out so well in a saree.'

Dharu blushed and said, 'I will, one more thing I want us to live together for a few months. Are you Ok with it?'

Aakash asked 'What are we doing from the past two weeks? We will continue the same for a few months.'

Dharu said- 'Now what I am going to ask is probably the most difficult one. I want us to take a month, long relationship break. Next month, the production house that I am working for is releasing the web series, so I will be going back to Bangalore. Let us have no contact for a month so that you can clearly take such a big decision.'

Aakash looked at her- 'Yes, you said it correctly, it will be very difficult but I don't think we can be away from each for so long. Anything else ma'am.

Dharu sounded playful and said- 'After 6 months of living together, we can get married, but I want a proper proposal. On your knees with a beautiful gold ring-it can be in private.'

'Ok, done' Aakash said with a smile.

16
No contact

Dharini reached Bangalore, she unpacked, quickly showered, ate a light meal and slept. She was so exhausted emotionally and physically that it did not take her more than 5 minutes to fall asleep. The next day she cleaned the house. That night too she fell asleep due to exhaustion. The third night, she visited her daughter, made back-to-back calls to her friends and relatives. She replayed the conversations till she fell asleep.

Problem started on the fourth day. Dharini started writing her novel, as soon as started writing some dialogues related to love, all memories of Aakash flooded in her mind. She somehow managed to complete the chapter and for two hours stayed in bed just remembering the time she spent with him. Break up, at any age was painful. Why did she have to be so thoughtful? Why couldn't she be selfish like so many other women? Once in her lifetime, true love had entered her life and she let it go because she felt that Aakash deserved someone better than her. She cried and felt better.

The following day, she decided to spend her time cooking whenever she was not writing. She decided to try some new recipes. She scrolled through different recipes but whenever she came across Shahi Paneer or Momos, she felt sad again as they were Aakash's favourite dishes. She decided to cook only South Indian dishes till she could heal from the broken heart. She put on a news channel on TV. A celebrity wedding was screened and the celebrity resembled Aakash. It was painful. How many times she had dreamt of Aakash as a Dulha. He would have been such a handsome bridegroom.

After that she went shopping. Usually shopping distracted her. But when she saw a handloom shop from Haryana, her mind was filled with his memories. Her heart actually ached and she was scared that she would probably die from a heart attack. Whenever she saw an Alpha male, her heart would ache.

1000 miles away in Mumbai, Aakash too was missing Dharini. But he was not as frustrated as her because he knew, he just had to wait for one month and she would be in his arms again. He did video calls with his son, partied with his friends and watched her pics and videos. He had clarity in his mind. It was Dharu or nothing.

Two weeks later, Dharu felt that she would go crazy. She had to hear his voice. He had blocked her on her request. So, she called him from a phone booth. She made a blank call like a teenager. All she wanted was to hear his voice.

'Hello, hello kaun hai'

'Mujhe malloom hai aap kaun ho'

When she heard his pleasant voice and felt he sounded alive and OK, she cut the call.

Two days later, she did another blank call.

'Hello, Hello kaun hai.'

'Dharu tum theek to ho na jaan'

Dharu could not control herself any longer.

'Hum theek nahi hain. I love you Aakash. I miss you. One month is too long.' After that, she started crying.

'I love you too Dharu. I will be in Bangalore this weekend. I knew how much you missed me when I read the new poem you had posted on social media. Even I can't be without you any longer.'

17

Mindo

It was a Saturday evening. Dharu and Aakash were enjoying a romantic candle light dinner. Dharu was lost in his eyes. His eyes twinkled even more in the soft candle light. They had ordered food and were sipping their drinks. The music also contributed to their silence.

It seemed as if their hearts were speaking to each other in a language only their hearts knew. These were the moments that reminded them that their love was buried deep inside their bodies-inside their souls.

Just when she was in this trance, she felt some blunt object poking her shoulder. She looked up and realized that the blunt thing was Maggie aunty's fingers.

'Hi, Dharu.'

'Hi Maggie aunty, how are you?'

'Your uncle and I were here to celebrate our wedding anniversary. Ok who is this handsome young man?'

'Oh! This is my friend Aakash and this is Maggie aunty.'

'Bye dear, your uncle must have started the car by now.' Then before she left, she whispered 'Friendo ki Mindo'.

All the healthy glow from Dharu's face vanished. Aakash immediately sensed that something was wrong.

'What did she say?'

'She asked me if you were my friend or my Mindo.'

'What a funny sounding word? What does it mean?'

'Mindo in Konkani means masculine gender of mistress. I am so sorry she called you this.'

'Ok, that's all. Why are you so upset then?'

'She is Maggie aunty-Margaret aunty, my step mom's best friend. Of all people, she had to see us together. She is the gossip queen of our community. Not only my step mom, but the entire west coast is going to know about this.'

'What west coast?'

'Goa to Cochin. That's where most Konkanis live.'

By then, dinner arrived- Kaju Paneer, Naan and Kashmiri Pulao. They ate quietly but this time without looking at each other.

When they reached home, they changed their clothes and were lying next to each other.

She turned towards him and pulled him towards her.

He said, 'Listen, if you are upset let's not do it.'

'Are you crazy? You have flown all the way just to be with me. I don't want you to ever regret this. All that you need to do is give me a delicious kiss and make me forget all my sadness. But only kiss won't do Ok.'

18

Step mom visits her

———❦———

Her doorbell rang the next morning at around 11 AM. After the meeting with Maggie aunty, Dharu knew that her step mom and her husband would visit her. Her step mom had married another man after Dharu's dad's death. Dharu shared a love-hate relationship with her step mom.

As soon as she came, her step mom looked at Aakash sarcastically, nodded her head and then spoke to her husband. 'You chit chat with this boy while I lecture my daughter inside.'

Dharu took her to her bedroom for the lecture. 'My dear girl I hope you get bored of playing with that beautiful toy soon.'

'Ma, he is a man, not a toy.'

'There must be a reason why they call such people toy boy. See, I understand you must be lonely but why a younger man. You need companionship at your age not romance.'

'He is a divorcee; he loves me and he needs my help in raising his son who is 12.'

'Are you crazy? If your father was alive, he would have said his favourite line- 'digging a canal and bringing a crocodile home.'

'Haven't you seen my life? Haven't you learnt anything from the fights we have had? Being a stepmom to a teenager is one of the most challenging roles. You were a teenager when your mother died and your dad married me. I know what difficulties I have gone through. Half the people really appreciate me for taking the responsibility of someone else's kids and the other half think I am a cruel step mom. Don't ruin the rest of your life for god's sake.'

'Ma but think again. For all the tough times you have been through, you have raised two girls who have become good and strong women. My sister is one of the best homemakers I have ever known and I am a successful writer. You were the first person to recognize my writing skills. You appreciated it. I used to think of you as a very artificial person when you would insist that I read novels and speak correct English. It is because of this insistence that I have a successful career as a motivational speaker and a writer today.'

Her stepmom's eyes filled with tears- 'Enjoy your name and fame. Make more money, write more and enjoy your life. Why do you want to get into the role of a wife and a mother again?'

'I want to continue the good deed that you did by being a stepmom. Maybe, I miss dad and you. I miss the family time we had Ma, the outings, the vacations, the fights, the parties and so many other things. These months after Tanya's wedding made me realize I am not the stay alone, stay single type. The bond I share with Aakash is the same kind that you and dad shared. We tend to show our love through care and concern rather than romance. We don't need words to express our love. I can literally feel the emotions that he goes through and so does he. He is a home bird and so am I.'

'I understand but stop being a romantic fool and think practically. Once you get fed up of his looks and his actions, you know what I mean, inform me. I will find you a nice person with a government job through my husband.'

'But ma, he is earning well, he is a techie with a good salary.'

'Whatever, said and done, he is in a private job with no job security. I will get you married to a government employee with adult children. So, no more arguments.'

Dharu knew that she could not argue with her but at the same time she also knew that she would never marry anyone other than Aakash.

Once they left, she asked Aakash what were he and her stepmom's husband discussing.

'Delhi politics.'

19
Sister sister

One Sunday morning, at 11, the bell rang. Dharu guessed who it could be. At the door were her sister and her husband.

She asked them to sit and asked if they wanted some tea but they refused. Her sister looked as if she was going to shout at her.

'Do you want to talk to Aakash?'

'Hi Aakash, I am not going to interview you. I have heard more than enough about you from two of my most trusted sources. She turned to Dharu and said- 'It's you who I need to talk to. Let's go inside.'

Inside the bedroom, both the sisters sat face to face on the bed.

'I don't have any intention of interfering in your personal life. I would have never come here when he is around.'

'What do you think about this?'

'He needs a mother and you need pleasure.'

'Please I love him.'

'You know what my elder one said the other day-Tanya Akka is so lucky. Dharu Mave is dating and I am sure she is going to live together with her boyfriend. What a cool mom she has.'

'Dharu, what kind of example are you setting for the next generation?'

'My dear baby sister the world is changing. Please come out of your kitchen.'

'I don't want to. If you were not my sister, I would have just stopped talking to you. Just marry him I say.'

'Ok, I will think about it.'

As soon as Dharu said this, her sister and her husband walked out of the house.

'My own sister is judging me now. She said that you need a mother and I need pleasure. Yuck.'

'Chill yaar, give her some time.'

But that was funny. I think I should seriously think about putting my name on the sugar baby website.'

Dharu laughed at this and then asked- 'By the way, what was Jiju talking to you about?'

'We were just discussing cricket. I think the problem is only with the women.'

'Ya, you are living their fantasy. I am sure they feel like telling you. Bro, go enjoy, no strings attached.'

20

meeting with daughter

It was almost ten on a Saturday night. Aakash and Dharu had finished their dinner when the phone rang. It was Tanya

'Hello Ma'

'Hello babu'

'We will be there in half an hour.'

'If you are missing me, come tomorrow morning. You are newly married. Nights should be for your husband.'

'And your nights Ma, for your boyfriend?'

'What are you saying?'

'I called Swathi, to wish her on her birthday. Spoke to her for an hour only about you. One of her lines about you was- Your mom is being naughty with a hottie. It seems you look 20 years younger. I can't wait to see my mom's hottie, so I will be there in half an hour.'

Dharu sat for five minutes and thought. Then, she repeated the conversation to Aakash. He was shocked. 'So, get ready for your surprise interview and I am sorry, it is going to be a tough one.'

'Do you want me to wear formals?'

'No, not required, that T-shirt is good but I think you need to change those shorts and wear track pants.'

'Sorry, no sexy satin night dress. Need to wear my gunny bag.'

'What?'

'Nightie.

'She has always seen me in nighties.'

When Tanya and Lucky arrived, Dharu pointed towards the sofa and said, 'Sit down'.

'No, we will sit at the dining table. Want to talk face to face.'

'First you,' she asked Aakash to sit and as soon as he did, Tanya sat on the opposite chair. After that Lucky sat down.

Dharu asked, 'Whiskey?'

'Yes aunty.' Said Lucky

'Wow, you have started drinking.'

'I started it two months after your wedding as I used to feel really lonely. So don't blame him for that.'

'Already defending him.'

After Dharu sat down, Tanya immediately started her questions.

Name-Aakash

Age-45

Dharu held Aakash's hand firmly as if to signal no matter what, she loved him.

Marital status- Divorced

Reason for divorce- My wife ran away with another man.

Dharu shouted- 'You are being really rude Tanya. You cannot ask personal questions to someone when you are meeting them for the first time.'

Aakash calmly said- 'It's Ok'

Kids-One son

Kid's age-12

Profession- Information Security Director.

Lucky said- 'Wow! That's something good.'

Why do you like her? – I think we have great chemistry.

Tanya looked at them holding hands and commented- 'I think it's more of biology here'.

Sensing the tense atmosphere, Lucky took 2 large sips of his drink.

'Sir, you seem to be a sensible man. What made you get interested in my normal and boring mother? Look at her, so ordinary, even her dressing sense sucks. You can do better than this. I find it strange that you like this Nightie Aunty.'

'Actually, I feel that she is anything but boring.'

'Are you one of those guys who are into older women?'

'No, I am not.'

'Ma, you better be careful. I think he is a player who has a checklist. After he dumps you, he will put a tick next to the option that says-date a mature woman.'

'Tanya, please you don't know him.'

'I didn't want to know him till now. I thought it was a monsoon romance with a toy boy. But he is here every other weekend. I think he is up to something.'

'How are you financially?'

'Tanya, even I haven't asked him this?' interrupted Dharu

Aakash just patted her hand as if to say he was alright.

'2 flats in 2 different cities. All EMI's paid. One education policy for my son. Alimony of 10 lakhs paid to my ex-wife as one time settlement. I think Lucky has already guessed what my salary is since he is also a techie. One life insurance policy, a pension fund, 5 acres of farm land in my village and some shares.'

'Ok if it's not her money then it must be her contacts. Do you want to become an actor or a writer?'

'No, I love my job'.

'You know Ma, let me be very frank here. He does not suit you. You need a Kavi in Khadi not a Techie in T-shirt. People are going to say what a mismatch'

Do you love her? Yes, I do

And so, do I. I forgive you for snatching her but if you ever hurt her, I will make your life miserable and I mean it.

Lucky took too more sips of whiskey while the others hadn't even touched their drinks.

'Will you marry her?'

'I can, right now, at this moment. But she says she needs more time.'

'What Ma, what's this? Is this some cheap publicity stunt of yours? Wait, I have to show you something. Swathi sent this to me.' Tanya took her phone, searched for something in it and showed a video of Dharu. The title of the video was- 'Romance writer's romance.' They were at a café and Aakash was kissing her on the cheek.'

'So much PDA, next time be careful. What is it ma, post menopause heightened sex drive?

'Shut up Tanya, don't talk to me like that in front of Lucky. Come to my room and you can shout at me as much as you want. Gentlemen help yourselves to some more pegs.'

'No, aunty I have to drive home.'

Tanya and Dharu were inside the room.

'Wow! Satin night dress. Let me remove that hair clip of yours.' As soon as she removed the hair clip from Dharu's hair, her thick curly hair fell over her shoulders.'

'You actually look good in this 90s wala haircut, ma. He has really changed you. Why don't you get married? Do you love him?

'Yes, I do. I want to prepare myself to be his son's stepmom. I want to make sure that Aakash really loves me and wants me.

Tanya cooled down and gave her mom a hug, 'Just want you to be safe and happy. Go enjoy yourself ma.

After they left, Dharu said, 'Aakash, I am really sorry for what happened today.'

'It is Ok Dharu, it is the love of a child towards it's mother that made her speak the way she did. I understand, I too love my mother.'

'What were you and Lucky talking about when we were inside?'

'He was asking if I had been to Australia. It seems he wants to settle there.'

'What? Ok, why should I get worried, he is an only child. I am sure his parents would never let him migrate so far.'

21

Meeting his ex and Ved

One weekend, Dharu had to visit a publisher in Delhi to get her book translated and published in Hindi. Aakash suggested that they should meet Ved. He spent the entire day with his son while Dharu was busy at the publishers. In the evening, Aakash, Ved and Dharu went to a fast-food restaurant. Over pizzas and burgers, Dharu observed Ved. He looked like a little version of Aakash. Not only his looks but also his gestures were like Aakash. The boy hardly smiled and was shy. Dharu also saw how just a few words of praise from them would light up the boy's face. It was proof enough to show that the boy did not receive enough attention from his parents at his home. Ved cried a lot and a few tears also were on Aakash's cheeks when it was time to say bye. Aakash dropped him at Soni's house.

That night, at around 9 PM, Soni and Saajan met them for dinner. Dharu had to admit that they were one of the best-looking couples, she had ever met but the most selfish too. They were hardly interested in talking about Ved and were busy taking pics to put on social media. Soni agreed to give full custody of Ved to Aakash which would happen after his academic year would end.

Once they reached Bangalore, Dharu said- 'Let us get engaged and start living together. I can't let a child live in such a toxic environment. His academic year is getting over in 6 months. Let us get married before he comes to Bangalore.

Aakash was thrilled. The next day, he proposed to Dharu in her house. He knelt on his knees and put a gold ring on her finger. Then he said the golden words- 'Will you marry me?' Dharu had tears of joy when she replied- 'Yes, I will.'

22
Living together and marriage

❤

Aakash moved in with Dharu. Best part of living together was they could have sex whenever they felt horny. They started to understand each other better. There were slight differences such as his discipline and her indiscipline but they learnt to live with it.

After a month, Aakash told Dharu that he had spoken about their relationship and marriage plans to his mother. His mother wanted to spend more time with Ved so she was planning to move in with them after the wedding.

Dharu said- 'Aakash, she is most welcome, who could be better than her for giving me guidance in bringing up Ved. She has raised such a wonderful person like you. I will have some good company too. We can gossip, make papads and pickles, have saas bahu fights, go shopping, go on pilgrimages and so on.'

'Are you sure you won't feel that there would be lack of privacy?'

'Aakash, are we in our twenties that we need privacy to do ghupa ghup all day. One hour of privacy in a day is enough, right? I want a proper family life.'

'I am so blessed to have you, Dharu.'

After six months, they had a simple Arya Samaj wedding.

23

Her first visit to his village

A week after their wedding, Aakash and Dharini visited his village. She was nervous. But his family seemed cordial. They gave the couple a warm welcome on the first day.

The next day was Karwa Chauth.

Aakash said, 'Dharu, you don't have to fast if you don't want to.'

'Aakash it is such a romantic festival. Food was my favourite thing till you entered my life again. It's OK, I am so excited about being here. Don't worry I will manage it.

When it was time to break the fast, Dharu was so happy. What she had seen in movies, she was actually doing it- watching his handsome face through the sieve and then him making her sip water to break her fast.

The next day, his sister's family came to visit them. Aakash felt that it was the right time to discuss property matters.

'I am going to give up my share of the property and both of you can divide my share equally.' He told his brother and sister.

Aakash handed a bag of jewels to his mother and said – 'Ma, keep these ancestral jewels that you had given to Soni. You can pass it on to whomever you want to.'

'Why?' asked his mother.

'Both of us are earning well. Whatever assets are in my name will go to my son and whatever is in her name will go to her daughter.'

Then he spoke to his brother and sister- 'You both have looked after Ma so far and you also take care of the land so you deserve to own the land.'

For the first time after their visit, Aakash's mother smiled at her wholeheartedly because she understood that the words were spoken by her son but the idea was Dharu's.

On the last day of their stay, Aakash took his brother's cycle, made Dharu sit on the pillion and rode to the fields.

It was a mustard field. First, he took her on the 'Machaan' and gave her a view of the fields. There was not a single person present on the fields. Once they came down, he ran to a small clearing in the middle of the fields and stood with his arms wide open. There was no one else around them. He screamed, 'Dharu come here'. Dharu was shocked to see this side of Aakash. Both of them did not like PDA but today he had become someone else. She ran towards him like a heroine in a 90s movie. She went straight into his arms and they stood silently like that for a minute. After that, Aakash said, 'Sorry no guitar and Topi'. Dharu blushed at this. Then he continued, 'Only this much is not enough.' Dharu was speechless and after that they made love under the open sky in the middle of a 'Sarson ka khet.'

'Cheeee, how will I go home. What will people think?'

It's OK. We will go through the backdoor. His sister-in-law was near the backdoor. He said- 'She fell down.'

His sister-in-law said in a naughty tone, 'She did not fall down, she was pushed. Your brother and I also have made a lot of backdoor entries when we were newly married. I will get your clothes Dharu and you can change here.

After she went to her room to get clothes, Dharu, whispered, 'I didn't know my goody goody husband could be so naughty.' Aakash winked, blew her a kiss and left.

That night, when they were leaving the village, his mother spoke- 'Aakash had told me you were happy about me living with you but now I am convinced that I can stay with you comfortably. Even though you are not one of us, you have touched our hearts. Now I know why Aakash was so stubborn about his decision to marry you. So can I live with you?'

'Of course, Maa ji, that is your house too.'

24

make me your muse

Soni, Saajan and their sons, arrived one weekend. There was a wedding they had to attend in Bangalore. Aakash's mother had gone to her village for two weeks. Dharu being the kind hostess, asked them to stay at their place. On Saturday evening, Soni and her sons decided to go down to the park. Ved asked Dharu and Aakash to join them. Aakash agreed but Dharu refused as she had to edit some parts of her novel and mail it. Saajan said that he had a headache so he wanted to take a nap.

Once, they left, Dharu went to her bedroom. She edited and mailed a portion of her novel to her publisher. Just as she was checking some fan mails in her mail box, Saajan entered the room and sat next to her on another chair that was beside the table.

'I have read all your books, watched all your web series and movies based on them. I have read your novels both in English and Hindi. I am a big fan of yours.'

'Thanks' Dharu said politely.

His voice became husky. 'Now I know why that bull is crazy about you. I saw your salsa video. You look so delicate and so flexible. Totally, at the mercy of that bull.'

Dharini understood where this conversation was heading. She pretended to do something on the laptop but actually had clicked the record button. She knew his eyes were on her breasts so he would not really bother about what she had pressed.

She observed that he was only wearing his vest and shorts. He held her hand in his. 'Your hands are so cold. I will make them warm. I want to make your whole body warm.'

'How lucky that bull is. First wife is a beauty and the second one is so mysterious. I used to always wonder what made that bull marry a woman whom no man would look at twice. It's not your looks. It's what you do to him.' He sighed.

'Look at me Dharu, look at this body of mine. Just imagine what I am capable of doing. Soni was a mother of a child when she came to me. Aren't you curious to know what made her leave everything and come to me?'

'I am not a bull. I am race horse, come ride me. Let's take this to the next level. What do want? Please tell me- hand cuffs, whips—make me your muse in your next novel. Promise me you will, every reader will go crazy reading about our adventures.'

'Soni and I have decided to open our marriage. She too feels that if she sleeps with Aakash, he will take better care of Ved. What a happy family we will be. The boys will grow up in an atmosphere full of love.'

'Tomorrow evening when they go to the park, we will do it. I will send some videos of mine. See for yourself, how my body is. I am sure after you see them, you will come running to me and say-Saajan take me. Wear that little black dress and that will give a hint that you want me.'

Finally, he left the room. Dharu was scared. She somehow calmed down and went to the kitchen and prepared some orange juice. She knew that after playing, the kids would be thirsty. She told herself, nothing was more important than Ved and she should not create more trouble in the kid's life. So, whatever she was planning to do, had to be done in such a way that it would not reach Ved's ears.

Dharu behaved as normally as she could after that. The next morning, Soni, her sons and Saajan went to the wedding. Aakash and she were alone in the house. She made Aakash listen to the entire recording. 'That sex maniac, I will murder him.'

'Calm down, don't let the kids know about this. This evening when you go to the park, make sure you return home in five minutes. You need to catch him red handed. Please hurry otherwise, I may end up getting raped.'

'Don't worry I will be here even before he takes one step towards you.'

'Aakash, do you think I should stop writing love stories. Do you think due to my writing, some men think I am a man crazy woman?'

'Are you out of your mind, Dharu? Writing gives purpose to your life just like Ved gives me purpose to my life. You inspire and motivate people through your work. I am sure you have come across at least 50 people who have told you that your work has influenced them or the people they know and has made their lives better. For every 100 good comments you get on your social media page, you will get 10 bad comments. Has that stopped you from writing? So even if a few men think of you as a man crazy woman, let them because nothing can change them. As far as Saajan is concerned, I have come to know from some of my friends that he is a 'tharkee'. Soni also knows this but she ignores it as she is only in love with his money and not him.

The next evening, Dharu wore her little black dress when she and Saajan were alone. He was in his boxers. She was so scared that she could hear her own heart beat loud and clear. As promised, Aakash arrived exactly five minutes later and rang the bell. Dharu ran and opened the door. Aakash closed the door, hugged Dharu and then punched Saajan on his face. He even slapped him twice? 'Kaminey meri ek biwi kafi nahi thi kya, ab doosri ke peeche pada hai.'

Saajan punched him back but Aakash bent down so he missed his punch. Dharu realised that with the body that Saajan had, he would crush Aakash easily so she screamed.

'Stop or I will send what I recorded to everyone I know'

'Randi, teri ye himmat' he tried to slap Dharu when Aakash held his hand and spoke so harshly in their native language that it made Saajan realize his mistake.

'We are forgiving you only because you are a father. Nothing can be more shameful for a man than his child having a bad image of him.'

'I am sorry Ma'am' Saajan apologized to Dharu.

'And also tell that wife of yours to stay away from my husband.' Said Dharu.

The next day, for the children's sake all of them behaved normally. Soni also knew about it and she had stopped flirting with Aakash. Finally, they left Bangalore. On that day, Dharu decided never to entertain Soni or Saajan again.

25

It was their first wedding anniversary

The day started with some good, morning sex. After that, several calls flowed from friends and relatives throughout the day wishing them 'Happy anniversary'. Time had flown so quickly in the past one year thought Dharu. So many changes had occurred. Ved had become a happy child. Aakash's mother was happier too due to Ved's happiness. Tanya and Lucky had moved to Australia. Dharu's step mom and sister realized that Aakash was a really good man.

Aakash's and Dharu's love for each other had increased and the passion between them remained the same. They were experiencing happy days again. Dharu realized that all this was possible only because she had decided to 'move on'.

Disclaimer

The characters and events depicted in this novella are fictitious. Any similarity to actual persons living or dead is purely coincidental.